Guess Who's Coming to Santa's for Dinner?

Guess Who's Coming to Santa's for Dinner?

Written and illustrated by

Tomie dePaola

SCHOLASTIC INC.

New York Toronto London Auckland Sydney
Mexico City New Delhi Hong Kong Buenos Aires

For Holly and Luigi,
who sent me a Christmas card that gave me the idea for this story.

And for all families everywhere
that could add their own stories about Christmas dinner to this one.

And, of course, for Bob, Anne, the Aussies and Mario,
who have all sat at MY Christmas dinner table.

ISBN 0-439-84243-3

Published by Scholastic Inc., 557 Broadway, New York, NY 10012,
by arrangement with G. P. Putnam's Sons, an imprint of Penguin Putnam Books for Young Readers,
a division of Penguin Group (USA) Inc. SCHOLASTIC and associated logos are
trademarks and/or registered trademarks of Scholastic Inc.

12 11 10 9 8 7 6 5 4 3 2   5 6 7 8 9 10/0

Printed in the U.S.A.   08

First Scholastic printing, November 2005

Designed by Marikka Tamura. Text set in Graham.

The art was done on 140 lb. Arches handmade coldpress watercolor paper using acrylics.

It was a few weeks before Christmas.

"You know, Mrs. C.," Santa said to Mrs. Claus, "I haven't seen my family in a while. Let's invite them all for Christmas dinner."

"Oh, my," Mrs. C. said. "Are you sure?"

"Oh, yes," Santa said. "I'm sure."

"All right, then. Make a list of who you want me to ask."

Santa got out his family photo album.

my sister, Sonja and her family

my sister, Olga

my friend, Lars

mistletoe

Tinsel

cousin Ulla

"I don't want to forget anyone," he said to himself.

The next morning, Mrs. C. went out to Santa's workshop.

"Do you have the list, Santa?" Mrs. C. asked.

"Here it is," Santa said.

"Oh, my," Mrs. C. said. "This is everybody. Are you sure you want *everybody*?"

"I'm sure," Santa said. "And I almost forgot. I want to invite my old friend Lars."

"Are you sure?" Mrs. C. asked.

Finally it was Christmas Eve. Away they flew!

Knock, knock. It was Santa's aunt Astrid.

On Christmas morning, the other relatives began arriving.
Santa's brother, Boris, his wife, Kirsten, and their children, Emma,
Emil, Erik and Baby Willie, arrived first.

Uncle Alfred came all the way from Bermuda,
where he had retired from ice fishing.

Cousin James B., a famous chef, came with his present.

Santa's sister Sonja, her husband, Bertie, and their children—
Lief, Lisbeth and the twins, Lina and Lukas—were right behind him.

Santa's older sister, Olga, was an opera singer. She marched in with her Italian piano player.

Cousin Ulla was the last of the family to arrive.

The door opened and in came Santa.

"Santa, you're back just in time. How was your trip?" Mrs. C. asked.

"Fine, fine," Santa said. "A bit of a fog over Antarctica, but we flew right through it."

Santa saw his family. "I'm so happy you are all here."

"If you'll excuse me," Mrs. C. said, "I'll just go out to the kitchen and finish cooking the dinner."

"We'll come and help," said Aunt Astrid, Sonja, Kirsten and Cousin James B.

"Oh, my," Mrs. C. said.

"Is the race on TV yet, Nick?" Boris asked Santa.

"Oh, no," Bertie groaned. "We don't have to watch those silly yaks racing around and around the Pole, do we?"

"Whadda ya mean, 'silly'! You got something better to do?" Boris shouted.

"Lots of interesting things. But then you wouldn't know anything about anything interesting," Bertie answered.

Finally everyone found a place to sit, and Mrs. C. served
Christmas punch. Uncle Alfred cornered Santa.

"Have I got a great invention for you, Nick. It'll be the
Christmas sensation next year. It's a combination, all-in-one
foot massager-back scratcher. Stand still while I strap it on you."

"Where's Lars?" Santa asked, looking around.
Lars rushed in.

"Make yourself at home, everyone!" Santa said.

COME TO THE PAGEANT AT FOUR
NO PETS ALLOWED, ESPECIALLY OSCAR

"Children, come with me! Let's go into the library. We are going to put on a Christmas pageant for the family before dinner."

LISBETH AND LINA, YOU WILL BE ANGELS.

ERIK, YOU WILL BE A SHEPHERD.

LUKAS, YOU WILL BE A SHEEP.

EMIL AND LIEF, YOU WILL BE A CAMEL. EMIL IN THE FRONT. LIEF IN THE BACK.

At four o'clock, Olga threw open the door and boomed:

"Come to the dining room, everyone! Dinner is ready,"
Mrs. C. said.

The children had their own table. Some of them didn't like it.

DINNER WAS A MESS!

TA-DAH!
MY FIERY FLAMING
PLUM PUDDING!
BAM!
IT'S A METEOR
SHOWER!
O-O-O-O-O!
GHRRR!
MEOW!
WOOF!

IT'S A SHOOTING STAR!
CALL THE FIRE DEPARTMENT!
NICK, WHAT GREAT FIREWORKS.
OH, MY!

Everyone slept late the next morning.

In the afternoon, the family gathered in the hall to hug and kiss and say good-bye.